The Purse People Adventures

By Abigail Dawn Rempel

and

Kimberly Dawn Rempel

Life is an adventure!! ☺

- Kim Rempel

- Abby Rempel

Table of Contents

Chapter One:
A Red Discovery

Ten year old Penny lived in a purse with her little brother. (Yes, you read that right.) They lived inside of a shiny pink purse. They were tiny little people you see – the size of a push pin - and fit perfectly in small places like purses and pockets. Never had they ever been caught – not by the giants who lived in the house, and not by Max the cat who was always on the prowl.

Penny and her three year old brother Spencer lived in the purse that happened to belong to a giant girl named Abigail. The giant did not know about the little people. Every once in a while Abigail would reach her hand into the purse to look for something, and surprise Penny and Spencer. Quickly, they would squish into a corner to hide. It was quite an adventure to live in a giant's purse...

The day began as it sometimes did, with giant Abigail stretched out on the couch, reading her favorite book. As the pink purse lay still at her side, Penny peeked out. Spencer poked his head out past the zipper too.

"What you doing?" Spencer said too loudly, like three year olds do.

"Shh!" Penny hissed. It was a miracle they hadn't been caught yet. Spencer was so loud. And clumsy too.

Penny was desperately tired of staying in the purse. She wanted to get out and explore. It was always better to explore at night while everyone slept, but she'd been cooped up in that purse with Spencer all day and couldn't wait another minute.

As she looked around the living room to see if it was safe to come out, she only saw Abigail, who seemed too busy notice them.

Penny swung one leg out, then the other. Spencer gasped and grinned as he also swung his legs over, toppled out, and followed her.

Just then, Penny stopped in her tracks. Spencer, not looking where he was going, bumped into her. She didn't seem to notice though. Something had caught her attention. In the corner of Abigail's pocket, some kind of red fluff stuck out. It was bright red, and curly too. A red fuzz on its own might not be that interesting. But then Penny saw it move! What would make a red fuzz wiggle?

Penny had to find out.

"Come on Spence," she motioned for him to follow her. They snuck over to the giant's pocket, careful not to be seen. The red fuzz had stopped wriggling now. Should they touch it? What could it be?

Penny slowly, carefully tiptoed up to the pocket and the fuzz. She stretched out her hand to touch it, and then it moved again. This time it wriggled and moved up, out of the pocket.

That's when they saw it.

As the red fuzz came out of the pocket, a face followed after it. The red curly fuzz was hair! And the face attached to it was that of a boy! The boy wriggled out of the pocket and climbed down. The whole time he watched Abigail carefully to make sure he would not be discovered. When he finally climbed down, he turned around and suddenly found himself face to face with Penny and Spencer.

"Ack!" the boy jumped when he saw them.

Penny and Spencer stood still like statues. They had never seen other little people before. The boy stood frozen for a minute too. Apparently he had also not seen other little people before. So there they stood, just staring at each other.

Finally, Penny spoke. "Uh, hi. I'm Penny." She smiled, "I didn't know there were others like us. What were you doing in there?"

"Oh," the boy smiled, "I've lived there for a long time. I think it's too small for me though. It's getting harder and harder to get in and out of there…" He ran his fingers through his bright red curls. "I was trying to get something out of there, but couldn't breathe anymore. Man, it's squishy in there."

Suddenly, giant Abigail reached her hand down to the purse. She moved it aside, and was about to roll over. The three stood next to her, and were about to be flattened!

Penny grabbed Spencer's hand and dove out of the way. Ethan dove too, and everyone collided in mid-air and landed in a pile. Abigail rolled over onto her side, covering the pocket Ethan had just come out of.

"You okay Spence?" Penny asked.

Ethan rubbed his head where he and Spencer had knocked together. The pocket was now hidden beneath the giant. She was lying right on it.

"I guess I won't be getting my stuff out of there for a while," Ethan said.

"I guess not," Penny said. "What were you trying to get?"

"Oh, uh -" Ethan looked around nervously, shifting from one foot to the other and back again. "Hey, is that Max?" Ethan pointed across the room.

Penny jumped and grabbed Spencer's hand, readying to run. "Where!?" Her eyes glanced above the piano. Under the TV stand. Over the edge of the couch. Max the cat was nowhere to be seen.

"I guess it was nothing." Ethan didn't seem at all frightened, and quickly changed the subject. "So where were you guys headed?"

Penny looked suspiciously at Ethan. Why didn't he want to talk about what was in the pocket? What was he hiding?

"Well…" She reluctantly answered, "We were going to explore. I've been in that purse all day and all night and I'm tired of it."

"You live in that purse?"

"Yes! Want to come see it?"

4

Ethan agreed, and they all made their way over for a tour.

Once inside, they climbed over some loose quarters and dimes and, being careful not to slip, sat next to each other on a big cherry lip balm.

"She keeps all kinds of things in here. Last week there was a sucker. We peeled back the paper just a little, and licked it. It was so good!" Spencer nodded and hoped another candy would be tucked inside the purse soon. He clapped his hands at the thought. Then, without his hands to balance him, he toppled over.

Penny ignored Spencer and looked thoughtfully at Ethan. He could be useful. She'd looked after Spencer by herself for a long time. Maybe he could help! "You know, you don't have to go back to that pocket. You could live here. There's enough space."

Ethan didn't have to think about it for long. He needed a new place to live.

"Sure, thanks! Where would I sleep?" Ethan asked.

"How about over there?" Penny pointed to the far corner.

"You want me to sleep on a marble?!" Ethan folded his arms across his chest.

"No, of course not!" Penny giggled, "You can sleep on the lint beside it."

"Oh." Ethan smiled and uncrossed his arms, "That makes more sense. You had me worried there for a minute."

Just then something bumped against the purse and shoved it off the edge of the couch. As the purse fell to the floor, Penny, Spencer and Ethan toppled all around. So did everything in the purse. The marble bounced around, clunking Ethan's head. Penny fell on top of Spencer, and then tumbled against the side. They shouted as the purse fell.

THUD! It landed on the floor.

The minute it hit the floor Max the house cat poked his head around the corner. Max was the only one who knew there were tiny people living in that purse, and he was eager to get his paws on them. He was certain they would be tasty treats. Max watchfully crept toward the purse, keeping an eye on Abigail all the while.

Inside the purse, everything was a mess. The three climbed out from under buttons and markers and other things that had fallen on them.

Penny lifted a seashell off of Spencer as he cried. "Aww, you okay buddy?" She hugged him as he sniffled.

While Ethan dusted himself off, he crinkled his nose as a terrible smell suddenly filled the purse. It was a rotten smell, like dead fish or sweaty feet. Then a dark shadow loomed over the opening of the purse, and they knew why. Max peered at them from above, breathing hot stinky cat breath all over them. He reached a black furry paw into the purse.

"RUN!" The three shouted, dashing away.

The paw swung at them. The claws slashed at the air. The three hid in a side pocket of the purse, safely out of Max's reach. The paw dug and swung some more, and then slipped out of the purse. Max's big green eyes stared into the purse, searching for them. Unable to spot them, he reached his paw in again, and swung and slashed.

Inside the pocket, Spencer bit his lip, holding back tears. Just then, Max's paw bumped up against the pocket. It surprised them all, and Spencer began to cry.

"Shh," Penny hugged him, "he'll go away soon Spence, but be quiet so he doesn't find us!"

The paw swung and dug, and then slipped out of the purse again. The green eyes stared in again. Penny, Spencer, and Ethan stayed perfectly still in the bottom of that pocket.

They waited for Max to lose interest and leave. They couldn't hear anything, but still they waited. They waited a long time. Finally, after a long, long wait, Penny peeked out of the side pocket. There was no paw swinging. There were no eyes peering back at her. Slowly, carefully, she climbed to the top of the purse and peeked out. The purse was still on the living room floor. Abigail was gone, and so was Max. The living room was quiet and empty.

Penny climbed back down to the pocket. "The coast is clear. He's gone."

Ethan and Spencer wriggled out of the side pocket, and everyone slumped on the floor, relieved.

"Phew! That was close!" Ethan said, running his fingers through his curly red hair. Spencer wiped away his tears and watched the top of the purse just in case.

"I just realized something," Penny said thoughtfully "You live with us now, but … don't you have any stuff to bring along?"

"Oh, sure." Ethan said, tying his shoe. He stopped, with his hands still holding laces in midair, and looked up at Penny. "We'll have to be really careful getting it."

Penny nodded. "Yes… it's dangerous no matter when we go. During the day, Max sleeps, but the people are sometimes home. At night, the people sleep, but then the cat is on the prowl…"

They both nodded and said nothing more. It would be a challenge to get Ethan's things. But then again, being the size of a push pin was a challenge every day.

Chapter Two:
Getting the Scroll

Ethan had agreed to leave the pocket he had been living in, and instead live with Penny and Spencer in the purse. Today was moving day. He wasn't sure about living with a three year old, but it would be worth it for all the room he'd have. He would not have to sleep crunched up like a ball anymore.

Ethan stood on the window sill, waiting for Penny to arrive. He watched the silvery moonlight shimmer on the leaves. He admired how the light sliced through the darkness. It reminded him of the scroll he'd left back in the pocket – the one he didn't want to tell Penny about. Today they would collect his things from the pocket, but how could he keep Penny from seeing the scroll?

It would soon be morning. They'd have to hurry if they wanted to finish before the people woke up.

"What are you doing, Ethan?" Penny called out as she approached.

Ethan startled out of his thoughts and turned to her with a smile. "I was thinking about how nice it will be to live in a place where I don't have to sleep all folded up." Penny smiled.

Spencer stared at them with wide, confused eyes. Why wouldn't he want to sleep folded up? Spencer liked it just fine.

"Do you have a lot of stuff to move in?" Penny asked, heading to the edge of the sill.

"I do have a book I'd like to bring. It's all about shipwrecks – like the Titanic. I love that book! I tuck it way in the bottom of the pocket so Abigail won't find it. I definitely want to bring that."

"Okay, let's go get it before everyone wakes up." Penny said, taking Spencer's hand.

From the edge of the sill, they stretched out their arms reaching toward the nearby lampstand. Penny went first. She wrapped her legs around the lampstand and slid down like a fireman on a pole. She landed solidly on her feet at the bottom, and waited to catch Spencer.

Spencer was helped onto the lampstand, and slid down. "Woohoooooo!" He slid fast, hardly hanging on, and landed PLOP into Penny's arms. He landed so hard, he almost knocked her over.

Once they were all down, they made their way to giant Abigail's room to retrieve the book about shipwrecks. Ethan was still not sure how he would bring the scroll along without Penny noticing.

On their way to Abigail's room, they all kept watch for Max. Max was huge, and fast too. The way his black fur glistened in the moonlight, it sometimes looked like a cape, which made him look even faster.

The problem with Max was that he loved to chase tiny things. Ethan and Penny guessed that if Max ever got a hold of them, he would eat them for sure. They couldn't imagine anything worse than being eaten by a cat. So they watched carefully. They never ever walked in the middle of a room where there was no place to hide. They stayed close to the edges, near furniture and other places they could quickly hide if there was trouble.

Suddenly, a button slid across the floor right in front of them. That meant only one thing – Max was close, and he was in the mood to chase things. A second later, Max darted into the room. He was heading for the button, but then stopped when he saw them.

Penny, Ethan and Spencer raced toward the nearby piano. Max was coming fast. The three slipped under the piano just in time. Max tried to stop on the slippery wood floor. His paws ran backward, but he couldn't stop. BAM! He smashed face-first into the piano. The three hid safely under the piano while Max sniffed and pawed to reach them. His hot, stinky cat breath panted near them, and they squished back farther. Max suddenly left, but the three kept watch, not knowing what would happen next.

Suddenly Max's paw stretched under the piano from the side. His claws were out, reaching and hooking, trying to snag one of them. He removed his paw, and stuck his nose under the piano. Then his eye. He watched them for a minute with that big, green eye, and then left.

The three stayed perfectly still for a whole minute, waiting for Max to try something else. They waited another minute, and another. After a long while, they heard the patter of his paws in the other room. They decided he must have gone back to chasing that button.

"That was close!" Ethan said, climbing out from under the piano. They all patted dust from their clothes, and eyed the room carefully. They could never be sure where Max would be.

Finally, all three made it safely to Abigail's bedroom. Here, they would find that pair of pants with the pocket where Ethan kept his things. They crawled under the crack of the closed door. Gentle moonlight shone in, and the only sound was Abigail's heavy breathing.

"Oh no," Penny sighed as she looked across the bedroom floor. It was littered with jewellery and pencil crayons and papers and crumpled clothing. Actually, it kind of looked a lot like the inside of the purse. "How are we even supposed to find that one pair of pants in this mess?"

Ethan grinned at Penny, and whispered, "Aw, don't worry about that. I found my pocket every night. I'm used to it. Plus, she always throws her pants in the same corner." He pointed to the farthest corner and waved for them to come. Penny held Spencer's hand and started walking. Spencer tugged his hand back and just stood there looking at the piles of clothes.

"What's the matter, Spencer?" Penny whispered, trying not to wake the giant.

"I no want to." Spencer crunched his eyebrows together, and spoke loudly, like three year olds do.

Abigail moved in her bed, and moaned sleepily.

"Shhh. You'll wake her! Or Max might hear! Whisper, okay?"
Spencer nodded and tried to whisper, but it just came out as
garbled squishy sounds. Apparently Spencer wasn't very good at
whispering.

While Penny and Spencer tried to figure out whispering, Ethan
continued on. This was his chance. Without them by his side, he
could grab the scroll, tuck it somewhere, and they'd never know.

He climbed over crumpled shirts and teddy bear legs, balanced
on pencil crayons, and snuck around hair clips until he finally
reached that one pair of pants in the corner. He opened the pocket
and wriggled all the way to the bottom. When he came back out,
he held in his hands the precious scroll, and his book about
shipwrecks. He hugged them to his chest, thankful to have them
back.

The scroll was about as long as his arm, and as thick as his wrist.
He flattened it and slid it up his pant leg to hide it. To keep it
from sliding out, he tucked one end into his sock. As he made his
way across the room to Penny and Spencer, the scroll felt weird
against his leg. He tried not to walk funny so they wouldn't
notice.

Then he heard it. When he would bend his leg, the scroll made a
crunching sound! That wouldn't work! He checked to see if
Penny was watching. She was still busy talking to Spencer, so he
turned around, took the scroll out of his pant leg, and rolled it up
into a little ball instead. It fit perfectly in his pocket. Well, there
was a bit of a bulge, but his shirt covered it pretty well.

When he got back, Penny and Spencer were still practicing
whispering.

"I've got it!" Ethan said.

"Oh good. Let's get out of here. This whispering thing isn't going very well." Penny said.

Spencer hissed out some more spitty sounds that were apparently supposed to be words. Ethan laughed. Penny shook her head, completely confused.

Suddenly Abigail's alarm beeped loudly. She bolted awake, and turned off the alarm. Max would arrive any minute now, just like every morning. The three needed to get back to the safety of their purse, and fast!

Chapter Three:
Adventure in the Mall

It was Saturday. The longest, hardest day of the week.

On Saturdays, giant Abigail was home, and so were her parents. It was not safe to explore, so Penny, Ethan, and Spencer had to stay in the purse all day. It was not very fun, but it was the only way to stay safe. It was afternoon now. They had been trapped in the purse all day, and everyone was starting to feel quite crabby.

All three sat at the thread-spool table, each coloring a picture on a tiny scrap of paper. Penny drew a princess with her pencil crayon nub. Ethan busily etched an image of the Titanic, again. He always drew ships. Spencer bent over his paper, with his tongue sticking out of his mouth as he scribbled furiously across his page. Suddenly they heard the door to Abigail's room burst open.

"Where is it? Where IS it?" Abigail hurried through her messy room tossing clothes here, and jewellery there. "Aha!" Abigail grabbed the shiny pink purse.

When the purse was jerked up quickly, Penny, Ethan and Spencer all went SPLAT face-first on the floor of the purse. They climbed out from under each other and scrambled to the zipper to see what was going on.

Penny reached the zipper first, just in time to hear a door slam. She peeked out. They were inside the van, and already pulling off the driveway. Ethan arrived at the zipper too, and pushed up against Penny as he tried to get a peek. Penny didn't like being so close. She felt like shoving Ethan away, but didn't, and chewed on her fingernail instead.

Giant Abigail was in the front seat, and her mom was driving.

"I hope they have a sparkly one. It will go great with my purse." Abigail said.

Her mom smiled, "It's the mall – I'm sure they'll have loads of selection. I'm proud of you for finally saving up enough to buy it."

So Abigail and her mom were on their way to the mall. Penny, Ethan and Spencer would have to be quiet, and stay tucked safely in their little purse. They knew it was not safe to explore in the mall – they could easily get lost. No, they would stick together, and wait in the purse until Abigail returned home.

"Oh well," Penny said as she closed the zipper, "it's kind of like exploring. Maybe we'll get an adventure after all!"

Ethan shrugged his shoulders and returned to his coloring. He wasn't sure being trapped in the purse would be any kind of adventure.

Penny and Ethan sank back down into the purse, where Spencer was lying on his back, apparently very bored.

"I wonder what she's going to buy?" Ethan wondered aloud.

Penny wondered too. But shouldn't she know? She'd been living in Abigail's purse long enough to know what she was like, and what kinds of things she wanted to buy. She sure didn't want to admit to Ethan that she didn't know.

"I'm more concerned about Spencer getting lost." Penny said, changing the subject. "We really need to stay in the purse now! No escaping. Even peeking out could be risky."

Unfortunately, Spencer didn't know about getting lost. He didn't understand that it was not safe in the mall. All he knew was that he didn't want to be quiet anymore. He was done staying in the purse.

While Penny and Ethan were talking, and he thought they were not looking, he pulled open the purse zipper and began to escape. Just as he was about to crawl out, two hands grabbed his waist and pulled him downward.

"I don't think so, sneaky!" Penny said, "You could get lost – then how would you ever get back home?"

In the mall, Abigail and her mom arrived at a store where the walls were hung full of rectangles and screens and cords. Both walked up to the counter, and started talking with the clerk.

"I'd like to buy an iphone," Abigail told the clerk. "Can you help me?"

The clerk showed her a few different models, and they talked about which one was best for her. She chose a phone, and then bought a pink gem-encrusted cover to go with it.

"Oh, it even matches my purse!" Abigail said.

Meanwhile, Penny was having a hard time keeping Spencer in the purse. He was definitely tired of being in there.

She plunked him onto a chair and gave him a raisin. "We're on our way home, but we're still in the mall – we really need to stay in the purse. Getting lost here would be the worst. Here – let's read Ethan's book about ships." She opened the book and began to read.

Spencer shouted and threw his raisin across the purse, hitting Ethan in the eye.

"Ow!" Ethan cried, holding both hands over his face.

"Spencer!" Penny gasped, and ran over to comfort Ethan.

Spencer dashed for the zipper, opened it, and crawled out.

Just then, the purse moved down like a high-speed elevator. Spencer clung to the purse handle, trying desperately not to fall off. The purse seemed to be falling to the floor.

Abigail set the purse down on the mall floor, and leaned over to tie her shoes. Spencer saw his chance, and jumped off of the purse. He'd made it! Finally, he was out!

Penny poked her head out of the purse and looked wildly around, searching for Spencer. She spotted him.

"Spencer!!!" She was lucky the noise of the mall crowd prevented Abigail from hearing her.

Spencer looked back to see Penny reaching out her hand and motioning for him to come. Suddenly he realized he had made a mistake and began to make his way back to the purse.

Suddenly the purse lifted up off the floor. Abigail had finished tying her shoes and stood to full height, bringing the purse up with her. Spencer watched as Penny rose up with the purse, far beyond his reach. She called his name the whole way up. How was he ever going to get back to Penny?

Penny and Ethan watched from the purse as Spencer shrunk from sight. They were horrified. How would they ever rescue Spencer?

Spencer's heart raced. The mall was full of people. He was surrounded by hundreds of legs and shoes and pant legs, all towering over him like skyscrapers.

Abigail started to walk away. Her long strides carried her quickly away, leaving him far behind. Spencer chased after her, but he was so small, and she was so large, and there were so many feet. Which ones were hers? And what would he do once he found them?

Spencer grabbed onto the shoelace of a runner headed in Abigail's direction. He hung on for dear life as the shoe followed. But it was moving too slowly. Abigail was getting farther and farther away. Before he could worry too long about it though, the runner he was on made such a sudden stop that Spencer was launched into the air.

He landed on the tile floor and rolled to a stop only inches away from Abigail just as she stepped up onto an escalator. What luck! There was a chance Spencer might be able to catch up on an escalator. He ran to the escalator as fast as his little legs could carry him. He was getting tired, but he had to get back to Penny.

The large, toothy steps moved away from him in waves. One step seemed to come out of the floor and move up, and another flat one followed, rising up from out of the floor, growing into a stair, and moving up. Abigail stood on a step about half way up. He had to hurry if he was going to catch her.

He climbed and ran up the escalator steps, struggling to not get stuck in the deep grooves. He was quickly approaching. He might make it before she got off the escalator and disappeared into the crowd.

Just when he was about to grab Abigail's pant leg, she stepped off of the escalator. Terrified, Spencer jumped at a pant leg closest to him, hoping it was the right one. With his hands, he clung to the bottom of the pants, and with his little feet he stood on the rim of the giant's shoe. He craned his neck to see the faces of the giants above. That's when he realized Abigail was walking away from him – he was on someone else's pants. Now what was he going to do?

Abigail proudly clutched her new phone in her hand as they left the store. Her purse swayed gently as she walked across the parking lot toward the van. Inside the purse, Penny and Ethan worried about Spencer.

Penny paced back and forth wondering aloud to herself. "What are we going to do?"

Ethan sat in the corner with his elbows on his knees and his hands on his face. He did not respond to Penny's questions.

"Well? Ethan, are you even listening?" Penny couldn't understand why Ethan was being so rude. Was he napping or crying or what? Why wasn't he answering? Didn't he care?

Ethan took his hands off of his face and looked up at Penny. "Sorry, no. I wasn't really listening. I -"

"I knew it. My little brother is lost and terrified, and you're busy napping."

"No, I really -" He tried to explain. He had been praying for Spencer's safety – that God would protect him and bring him back home somehow. But Penny was too upset right now. An explanation would have to wait.

"Just help me figure this out, will you? We need to -"

Just then they heard the van door slam. They looked at each other with stunned faces. Were they in the van already? Had Spencer made it? They scrambled for the zipper.

Penny jerked the zipper open, not being careful Abigail wouldn't see them. She poked her head out, and Ethan arrived and poked his head out too. They craned and searched, but couldn't see Spencer anywhere.

The van pulled away, leaving the mall behind.

Ethan's eyes glistened. He sniffed and disappeared into the purse.

Penny couldn't believe it. Spencer had been left behind. She would probably never see her little brother again. A tear slipped down her cheek as she started to climb back down into the purse.

Suddenly something grabbed her hand. Penny looked up and could not believe what she saw.

"HI!" Spencer grinned as he held Penny's hand.

"Spencer!" Penny pulled him into the purse and wrapped both arms around him. "I'm so glad you're okay!" She hugged him tightly like she might never let go.

Ethan smiled and wiped a tear from his eye. "You made it! How did you find your way back Spencer?"

"I was on the mom's pants!"

"Oh!! And she brought you right here into the van with us!" Penny said. Then, after a thoughtful pause, she looked at Spencer seriously. "You know, you could have gotten left behind. I thought you were lost."

Spencer's smile disappeared, and he hung his head. A tear fell from his face and splashed on his shoe. "Sorry" he said.

Penny hugged him again. "I know buddy. It's really important to listen when I tell you stuff, okay?"

He looked up and nodded, promising to always sit still when Penny tells him too. Well, he'd really try.

Just then, the purse zipper opened and a huge rectangular thing was lowered into the purse. It was long and took up a lot of space. As they looked it over, they realized it was Abigail's phone! She had tucked it into the purse.

Penny pressed her hands on the screen, and started tapping and sliding icons until she came across something amazing. There were games on this phone! Ethan, Penny, and Spencer took turns blasting bubbles and racing cars on that pink sparkly phone.

If they were lucky enough that the phone might be left in the purse with them on Saturdays sometimes, being stuck in the purse all day would be much more exciting from now on.

Chapter Four:
Ethan's Lucky Day

"Come on Abigail, time to go! Get in the car please!" Giant Abigail's mom called down the stairs. Abigail jumped up from her bed where she had been lying reading a book.

Penny and Ethan were inside the purse. When they heard the mom call, they looked at each other, worried. Would Abigail take the purse with her to town? The last time they had gone to town, it had not gone well. Spencer almost got lost in the store.

Ethan and Penny peeked out of the purse, hoping she would not scoop them up. They watched Abigail dash around her room. She grabbed a notebook, rummaged through a drawer and finally came out with a pencil. She looked around the room, searching for something. Was she looking for her purse?

Finally she left the room, leaving the purse behind.

Relieved, Ethan looked at Penny and smiled. "I plan to explore. Want me to bring anything back for you?"

Ethan and Penny had worked out a system of taking turns caring for Spencer. Today was Penny's day to watch him, which usually meant staying close to the purse. Today, Abigail was at school, which meant her iphone was at home.

Penny pressed a button on the phone, and the screen lit up. "I think we have everything we need right here."

Ethan nodded and climbed out of the purse, closing the zipper behind him.

"Remember to stay out of sight!" Penny called after him.

Ethan kept to the edge of the livingroom. He didn't know what he was looking for, but he'd know it when he saw it. He felt like one of the explorers he read about in his sailing books. They were always discovering new things and searching for lost treasure.

That's when he spotted something shiny in the middle of the room. He couldn't tell what it was from that distance, but it was round and glimmered just like a treasure would.

The mysterious gem was in the middle of the room, far away from everything. Max was nowhere to be seen, but it was still a risk. If Max would suddenly appear – and he did that sometimes – Ethan would be in trouble. This was dangerous indeed.

Sunlight glinted off the silver circle. Ethan decided he had to find out what it was, no matter the danger. He silently prayed for God's protection and ran across the room.

It was a long, terrifying run to the middle of the room. As he ran, he watched out for Max. Finally he came upon the shiny round object. It was as wide as he was tall, and had a bumpy edge all the way around, like a gear. On the flat surface was an embossed image – almost like a carving – of a big ship with sails. Beneath the ship was written, *10 cents.*

He couldn't stay to examine it though. Max could be anywhere. He had to get the dime home, but how? It was too tall and heavy for him to carry.

Then an idea came to him. It was a dangerous idea. If he could lift the dime up onto its side, he could roll it. This would be tricky. It could also be noisy against the wood floor and attract Max's attention. He admired the big ship with all its sails and decided it was worth the risk.

Bending down, he hoisted the dime up. It was heavy! His hands felt like they might fall off from the weight of the dime. He kept lifting and pushed it all the way until it was upright. It stood as tall as him. With both hands holding the dime in place, he stopped to catch his breath. Then, looking around again for Max, he began rolling it toward the edge of the room. It made a rumbling sound as it rolled.

He didn't make it more than a few steps before Max appeared in the doorway. Ethan couldn't stop the dime from rolling and making noise, so Max caught sight of him instantly.

Ethan's heart was pounding now, not from the work of moving the dime, but from fear. He was still in the wide open middle of the room. How would he escape? He had to think fast.

Max lowered his body, preparing to pounce. Ethan shoved the dime forward as hard as he could, and ran for the couch. The dime rolled toward an armchair, rumbling and shimmering all the way. Ethan dashed toward the couch.

Now there were two things to chase! Ethan hoped Max would go after the dime instead, but didn't wait around to find out. Max bounded across the room in hot pursuit, his green eyes wide and hungry looking.

Max was gaining on Ethan. Ethan was nearing the couch, but he could feel Max's hot breath already. He prayed. He ran. And, at the last possible second, just before Max could bite him, Ethan dove through the air and slid under the couch. BUMP Max's face hit the couch. Ethan was safe.

Panting heavily, Ethan scooted further back under the couch. Just then, Max lowered his face to the floor and stared at Ethan with his big green eyes. Then his eyes disappeared, and his paw reached under the couch. His sharp claws swiped, trying to catch Ethan, but couldn't quite reach.

He swiped and peeked under the couch, and then swiped some more but he just couldn't reach Ethan. Finally the black paw withdrew, and Max couldn't be seen anymore.

Ethan knew better than to think Max had gone. Probably, the cat was sitting on the couch waiting to pounce. He would have to stay under the couch now for a long, long while until Max thought he'd escaped somehow.

While he waited, his thoughts wandered back to his scroll. Since the day he'd moved into the purse he had kept it hidden from Penny. He didn't think she would understand how the words on that scroll could be so precious to him. Still, he did want to share them with her. The words might become precious to her too.

Meanwhile, Penny and Spencer had played games on the phone, gone for a pleasant, though cautious walk, and had just finished coloring. They were just about to sit down for a snack when something caught Penny's eye. Some kind of paper was sticking out from under Ethan's bed.

She handed Spencer a raisin. "Huh. What's that?" She asked, taking a bit of raisin herself.

Without looking up, Spencer answered. "My raisin," and took another bite.

Penny walked over to Ethan's bed for a closer look. A curled paper end poked out from under his blanket just enough so she could see it. It looked a little like a tube. Or a scroll. Or maybe a map.

"Spence, did Ethan ever show you this paper?" She kept staring at it while she spoke.

Spencer clumsily tried to get off the bench, but fell to the floor in a heap. BOOF. Without a word, he got up, and came to her side to look at the curious paper too. He shook his head and reached a sticky hand to grab it.

Penny grabbed his hand. "No Spence, we can't do that. It's Ethan's. Don't touch it, okay?"

Spencer jerked his hand away, crumpled his eyebrows at her, and marched back to the table to finish his raisin.

But, Penny thought, *if it would accidentally unfold…* She kicked at it with her foot.

The paper wiggled, but didn't unroll. Penny looked back at Spencer. His back was turned. She kicked it again, harder this time. The paper wiggled and made a rustling sound.

At the sound, Spencer whipped his head around. "No touching, okay!" He said loudly with angry eyebrows.

Penny's cheeks turned pink. "Okay, okay. We won't touch it. Oh, but I'm just so curious!" She looked at Spencer, almost wishing he'd say they should open the paper.

"No touching." He nodded firmly, and finished off his raisin.

Penny sighed and sat down at the table. "I know…"

Ethan had waited long enough, he thought. Max should have long been gone by now. He gazed across the room, hoping to see where the dime had rolled to. He had pushed it toward the armchair, but – oh! There it was, leaned up against the foot of chair. It would be a long, hard, dangerous trek across the house with that heavy dime, but he didn't care. It would be worth it to be able to admire that silver ship every day.

An idea came to him. He snuck out the back of the couch, edging carefully around the room. Max was nowhere to be seen. Ethan tiptoed to the armchair and arrived at the dime. He'd made it, but how was he going to get the dime back to the purse? Even if he could roll it all the way there, the noise would alert Max right away. He had to figure out another way.

"Aha!" Ethan snapped his fingers.

He checked for Max again, then climbed up the armchair leg and squeezed under the cushion. After a few seconds of crawling around in there, he came out again with a long strip of white paper – part of the armchair's tag.

He made his way back to the dime. Carefully, the dime was laid on one end of the paper strip. Ethan grabbed the other end, and pulled it silently across the floor like a sled. Max would never hear the rolling dime this way!

Smoothly, quietly, and very cautiously, Ethan hauled that dime back to the purse, very pleased with his newly discovered treasure.

Chapter Five:
Penny's Birthday

Ethan cornered Spencer under a desk, and growled, wriggling his claw fingers.

"Mwah-hah-ha! Now I've got you!" Ethan said in a monster voice.

Spencer wriggled and laughed and screamed all at the same time while he tried to get away. Suddenly Spencer launched himself at Ethan, wrapping himself around his leg like a monkey. Ethan tried to shake him off, and pull him off, but Spencer could hang on like crazy glue. Ethan tugged and pulled and tried so hard to get Spencer off of him, but he fell. Spencer took the opportunity, and climbed up and parked himself on Ethan's chest.

"Got YOU!" Spencer smiled. Ethan grinned back, surprised and panting.

"How on earth did you win? You're THREE!" Ethan couldn't believe he'd lost to a three year old.

Meanwhile, Penny was off exploring in the kitchen, looking for food. Her steps were quiet and her glances sneaky, as she tried to avoid the cat. Penny peeked tentatively out from behind the toaster on the kitchen counter and edged closer to the edge.

Armed with a rope, a thumb tack, a paper clip, and a button, she was ready for anything.

Penny surveyed the scene and noticed the cat sleeping soundly on the rocking chair in the living room. Abigail's dad was already at work by this time of day, and her mom had just left through the kitchen door to drop Abigail at school. Everything was going according to plan.

It would be easy for Penny to slide down the electrical cord of the phone to get to the floor. From there she could run over to the pantry, grab some bread and maybe a piece of granola bar. If she was lucky, she'd find a side of cheese for their breakfast.

There was just one problem. The cat was starting to twitch.

Penny swallowed hard, and reached for the cord. She slid silently down the cord. She ran along the edge of the cupboards being sure not to make a sound. Just as she neared the pantry, the house door slammed, waking the cat. Penny ran at top speed for the last twelve inches to the pantry, and hid behind the dustpan.

Back at the purse, Ethan and Spencer were munching on bits of carrot. Ethan looked over at the calendar and saw a red circle drawn on today's date. Curious, he went to inspect. Inside the circle, the words, "My Birthday" were scrawled in red pen.

"Hey! It's Penny's birthday today! And she never even said anything, the sneak…"

"Birthday Party! We eat cake?" Spencer said around a mouthful of carrot.

"Well, we should do something, shouldn't we?" Ethan walked back and forth as he thought, and took another bite of carrot. "What does Penny want?"

Suddenly he stopped. Something was different. He walked over to his bed and pulled the blanket up. The scroll looked like it had been moved.

"Spencer?"

Spencer walked over to Ethan, who was still holding up the blanket.

"Were you playing with my stuff?" Ethan asked.

Spencer bunched up his eyebrows playfully and wagged a finger at Ethan. "No touching! We no touch Ethan paper."

"Well someone moved it." Then a terrible thought came to his mind. What if Penny had moved it? Or worse, what if she'd opened it and read it? Would she just go through his stuff like that?

"Wait – what do you mean "*WE* no touch"? Did Penny open it?"

Spencer shook his head with bunched up eyebrows. Then he said, "She do this." And he tapped the scroll with his shoe.

"Hmm." Ethan became thoughtful. So she was curious. And she also respected his privacy. Maybe she would like what was written on it after all. The ancient words were precious to him, but maybe he could risk sharing them with her.

"I've got it!" He said it so forcefully, carrot bits flew out of his mouth. "I know JUST what to do!" Ethan reached under the bed and pulled out his precious scroll. "Today, for her birthday, Penny will do what she wanted to do – read this scroll."

It was a scary thought, but the ancient words themselves gave him courage.

Penny was still hiding behind the dustpan when suddenly the mom strode into the kitchen. She grabbed her coffee mug from the counter and muttered, "Good grief! I don't have time for this today!" Then she turned and left the house again.

Whew. That was a close one, thought Penny. Her relief was short lived because just as she exhaled, she could see the cat approaching the pantry. Panicked to find safety, Penny looked around for a hiding spot.

Her best option was to run and hide behind the bag of rice on the floor only a short distance away. But she had to wait. She had to be sure it was worth the risk. If she ran now the cat would certainly get her, but if he didn't know she was there, it would be better to stay still.

The cat sniffed at the pantry door, his breath hot and smelly. Penny was ready to bolt, but in a moment of brilliance she decided to throw her button like a Frisbee across the kitchen floor. It worked, the cat followed the button, allowing Penny to hide behind the bag of rice until she was sure the coast was clear.

She ducked into the pantry, and began the search for food. Moments later she emerged with a piece of bread and a couple of raisins to share with the boys. She peeked around the corner to check for the cat. Max was at the opposite end of the room, batting the button around. She took her chance, and snuck away, carrying the bounty home.

When Penny arrived home she slid the zipper back. As soon as she opened the purse, Spencer and Ethan shouted,

"SURPRISE!!" Penny jumped.

"Happy Birthday!"

Before Penny could say anything, Ethan said, "We have a gift for you."

"Oh?" Penny smiled and set down the cheese and raisins. "What is it?"

Ethan's hands were behind his back as he spoke. "Well, I understand you found my scroll and were curious about it."

Penny looked sideways at Spencer. Why did he always have to blurt everything out? It was impossible to keep secrets with a toddler around.

Ethan continued, "And I appreciate that you didn't sneak a peek."

Penny smiled sheepishly. Little did he know. She probably would have if Spencer hadn't said something.

"This scroll has been very dear to me. What is on it is precious and important. It's helped me be brave." Ethan swallowed hard.

Was he doing the right thing? Yes, he would be courageous. He would show her.

"Here," Ethan's hands held out the scroll to Penny, "I want to share this with you."

Penny's mouth parted in a surprised smile. Twenty different thoughts ran through her head all at once. Ethan loved stories of pirates and sea explorers – maybe this was a treasure map! Or a clue! Or maybe it was a special object he'd found in the house one day. Oh, what could it be? She was about to find out.

She reached out and gently took the scroll. It felt light and smooth in her hands. "Thanks Ethan."

The scroll was slowly unrolled. Ethan swallowed nervously. Penny's eyes grew large. Spencer busily colored on the wall of the purse while no one was looking.

Finally, the scroll laid open. There was no map. There were only words that read:

BE STRONG AND COURAGEOUS.
DO NOT BE AFRAID OR DISCOURAGED
FOR THE LORD YOUR GOD IS WITH YOU
WHEREVER YOU GO
JOSHUA 1:9

Penny looked at the words but said nothing.

"So? What do you think?" Ethan asked.

"Uh…" Penny tried to hide her disappointment. She had really hoped it would be a map or something adventurous or fun. But it was just a bunch of words she didn't understand. "Uh… I just… what does it mean?"

Ethan was confused. He thought the words were quite clear. "It means God is with me wherever I go, so I don't have to be afraid or discouraged. It means I'm never alone and that he's always taking care of me."

"Oh." Penny shrugged her shoulders and rolled up the scroll. "That's nice." A sigh escaped as she handed the scroll back to Ethan. "Thanks for showing me."

Ethan tucked it back under his bed. Had he made a mistake showing it to Penny? She didn't seem to care about the words or what they meant to him. Why didn't she understand?

The two were so busy thinking about the scroll they didn't notice Spencer had drawn swirls and stick people across the bottom of every wall of the purse. He'd even begun drawing on himself. There he sat, surrounded by crayons and decorated with swirls on his arms and a moustache on his little face, very satisfied with himself. His tongue stuck out of his mouth as he drew another picture on his bare foot. He had never had so much fun.

Chapter Six:
The Creatures In the Tunnel

Today Max was gone. He had been taken to someone else's house while Abigail's family was on vacation. Finally Penny, Ethan, and Spencer would have freedom to roam the house without fear. Even with clumsy, loud Spencer, they could walk freely in the house.

The fact was they had no choice but to roam throughout the house because Abigail had taken her purse with her. Thankfully, they'd been left behind in the house so they wouldn't have to risk losing Spencer again.

It was on this third day of their exploration they came across something curious. There, behind the dryer in the laundry room, was a hole in the wall. They had never noticed it before. Of course, they had never really ventured into the laundry room before. It was at the farthest end of the house, so they'd never bothered.

"Do you think anything is in there?" Ethan asked as they approached the hole.

Spencer had run ahead and was already poking his head into the hole. "HELLOOO!!!!" he shouted.

"Shh! Spencer! Don't do that!" Penny said.

Spencer looked back at her. "Why?"

"Well – What if – I – I don't know. Just don't." Penny said, putting her hands on her hips.

They gathered around the hole, each trying to peer inside. To their surprise, they discovered a long cave-like tunnel. Medieval torches hung from the walls and lit the corridor as far as they could see.

"Whoa…" Ethan said. His heart pounded. He had only read about such caves. He never dreamed he would ever get to see one.

"Oooh! C'mon guys, let's check it out!" Penny climbed into the tunnel and grabbed a torch.

Spencer reached for a torch too, but it was just beyond his grasp so he jumped and bumped it out of its holder. It was about to tumble down onto his head when Ethan caught it just in time.

"I don't think so, Spence. I'll hold it for you though." Ethan said.

Spencer really wanted to hold the torch, but agreed.

They walked slowly and quietly down the corridor. As they moved, the flames flickered and sent their shadows dancing in all directions across the cave walls and floor. An occasional groan, gurgle, and buzz echoed through the cave.

"What was that?" Ethan asked nervously. If the shadows weren't scary enough, the weird sounds definitely were.

"I – I don't know." Penny's voice trembled, but she tried to sound brave. She had to stay strong so the boys wouldn't be afraid. It was hard though because she was scared too, just like them.

"What if someone – or something – lives in here?" Ethan wondered out loud, "I mean, what if a rat lives in here? What if he hates strangers? Especially strangers that take their torches without asking? --Or what if it's a snake's tunnel?"

"Dragon?" Spencer asked.

"Yes – what if it's a fire-breathing snake?" Ethan said.

"ROOOOOAAAARRRR!!!!" Spencer's shout echoed through the corridor. He froze in position, with his hands in a claw shape, suddenly afraid of his own echoed words. Suddenly he realized there really could be a scary monster in there with them. Spencer hurried to walk closer to Penny.

"Ooo-kay. I think we're getting carried away. There are no snakes or rats or fire-breathing anythings in here. Just us." She said it, but she didn't really believe it. What if there were big, scary creatures in that tunnel with them? There was nowhere to hide – how would they escape? She chewed her fingernail as they continued through the tunnel.

Just then, Penny spotted a small door up ahead. It was wooden, arched, and had a tiny little handle on it.

Penny stopped. "Hey," she whispered, "look at that."

Spencer poked his head out from behind Penny. "What is dat!" He asked loudly.

"Spencer! SHHH!" Penny hissed at him. Why couldn't this boy whisper?

All three crept closer to the door. As they neared, they saw a faded plaque that hung on the door. Ethan came close to read it.

"Mr & Mrs"

Ethan slid his fingers across the words. "Hmm. There was more written here, but it's faded away."

Spencer reached up to feel the letters too. "Faded," he repeated.

"Well, it's clear a couple lives here. And they're small enough to fit in this door, so they're close to our size... should we knock and find out who it is?" Penny asked.

"I guess." Ethan shrugged.

Penny nodded and knocked on the door.

Suddenly goosebumps spread across Ethan's arms and legs. "Wait - what if it's two snakes?"

But it was too late. They had already knocked. Ethan looked around. The tunnel was straight and long – they would have no chance of outrunning a pair of snakes. Especially if they did breathe fire. He looked down at Spencer who was watching him. He smiled, trying to look brave and happy so Spencer wouldn't worry.

Inside, they heard scratching. Did snakes scratch? Then the door swung open.

A pointy little nose poked out into the hall, and the little grey mouse said, "Hello?"

Penny and Ethan smiled and sighed with relief. Neither one had ever been so happy to see a mouse before.

"Hello!" Ethan and Penny answered in unison.

"May I help you?" The elderly mouse smiled and looked at them over her wire glasses. Her yellow dress nearly touched the floor, and its red polka dots matched perfectly with the red bow in her hair.

"Oh. I don't know. We're just glad you're not an angry fire breathing snake!"

The kind looking mouse chuckled, "No, I'm definitely not a snake. And I have never breathed fire either!" What are your names?"

They introduced themselves, and she said she was Mrs. Mouse. She lived with her husband Mr. Mouse, who was busy making some biscuits in the kitchen.

"They're nearly ready - would you like to come in and have some?" She opened the door wider, and the smell of fresh baked cheese biscuits wafted into the tunnel.

Ethan and Penny hung their torches in two empty holders in the hall, and the three entered the Mouse's home. They tried to be polite, but they were very hungry and the food smelled so good. They walked quickly to the table where Mr. Mouse greeted them.

"Oh, hi!" He wore a white apron over his vest and blue-striped shirt. He smiled and dusted flour from his his necktie as he carried a tray of fresh biscuits to the table, "You're just in time!"

Everyone sat at the large wood table and enjoyed warm, tasty biscuits with their new neighbors.

Ethan looked around the Mouse's home while he chewed. The living area had a round woven carpet in the middle of the floor, on which two wooden rocking chairs sat. A coffee table stood in the middle of the room, and a thick, white book lay closed on top of it. The book reminded him of some of the history books he'd seen or read about – the kind treasure hunters would use to track down clues to buried treasures.

Ethan turned his attention back to the table to hear Penny describing their frightening journey through the tunnels.

"Ethan was worried about what kind of creature lived in here."

"Yeah, so?" Ethan said, looking sharply at Penny. "It's normal to be afraid you know. Everyone feels scared sometimes – even if they try to pretend they're not."

Before they could argue, Mrs. Mouse spoke. "You're right Ethan, fear is normal. So let me ask you something."

Ethan swallowed a piece of warm biscuit and waited for the question.

"You were afraid in the cave, but kept on going. You could have turned and ran home, but you kept going. That's bravery."

Mr. Mouse nodded, "Absolutely."

"How did you have the courage to do that?" Mrs. Mouse asked, taking a sip of tea.

"I don't know." Ethan shrugged and became thoughtful. Then he remembered his scroll's ancient words that had given him courage all these years. The fact that the all-powerful, loving God of the universe was right there with him all the time made him feel pretty safe no matter where he was.

"I guess I can be brave because I know I'm not alone."

Mr. and Mrs. Mouse looked at each other in surprise. "Isn't that fascinating…"

Mrs. Mouse rose from her chair and left the dining room without a word. Mr. Mouse leaned back in his chair and folded his hands across his chest as he told a story.

"Last month Max almost got me," Mr. Mouse began. "I had made the mistake of hiding behind the toaster. I was cornered, and Max knew it. No matter which way I would have tried to run, he would have caught me."

Penny, Ethan, and Spencer each leaned forward with wide eyes as they listened.

Mr. Mouse continued, "I thought I was a gonner. All I could do was crunch up in a little ball, and hope that Max didn't have the smarts or the strength to move that toaster. Max was going to get me, I was sure of it. I was afraid alright, but I knew something that Max didn't know -"

Just then Mrs. Mouse returned to the table with a picture frame in her hands. She laid it on the table and Mr. Mouse picked it up.

"This." Mr. Mouse held the frame against his shirt so no one could see what the picture was. "This was what I knew that Max didn't. And because I knew it, it gave me courage."

Mr. Mouse turned the frame around to show the three. There, in tiny stitched lettering, were the ancient words Ethan knew so well.

BE STRONG AND COURAGEOUS.
DO NOT BE AFRAID OR DISCOURAGED
FOR THE LORD YOUR GOD IS WITH YOU
WHEREVER YOU GO
JOSHUA 1:9

"No way!" Ethan whispered to himself.

"You know these words then?" Mr. Mouse asked, passing the frame to Ethan.

"Yes! I have these words on a scroll under my bed. They've always given me comfort, especially when I'm alone or sad or scared." Ethan reached to take the frame from Mr. Mouse, and ran his fingers across the intricate stitching.

"Wait a minute," Penny said, crunching up her brow, "How did those words help you when you were about to be eaten by Max? It doesn't make any sense."

Mr. Mouse nodded. "Good question. The words reminded me that even there behind the toaster, God was with me."

Penny still looked confused, so Mr. Mouse tried explaining another way.

"It's kind of like… well, have you ever hidden from Max in a very safe place?"

Penny thought for a moment. "Yes. When we dove under the piano that time Max was chasing us, we were safe under there. He couldn't get us at all."

"Yeah!" Spencer said, "Max went SPLAT!" He slapped his hands together in a loud clap.

Mr. Mouse chuckled. "Ah, good. Okay, the piano. So, knowing God is with me is like hiding under the piano. Even though there is danger and reason to be afraid, the piano protected you, so you didn't need to be afraid."

51

Before Penny could respond, a loud rumbling sound filled the house and the table began to shake. The floor and walls began to shake too.

"What is dat!!?" Spencer shouted. They all looked wildly around the Mouse's home as it shook.

Then Mr. Mouse stood and raised his hands in the air. "I think I know what this is!" he shouted over the loud rumbling. "I think it's their fridge – it's been doing this for the last two days. It should stop in a minute."

The tea cups and biscuits wiggled on the table. Everyone stood, looking around at the walls, and holding the person next to them.

Then, as suddenly as it began, the sound stopped. They stood in silence for a moment before anyone spoke.

Mrs. Mouse adjusted her crooked wire glasses. "Oh my!"

"That was a loud one." Mr. Mouse said, returning to his chair. "You alright?" He asked the three.

Their eyes were wide and they still clung to each other, but slowly returned to their chairs, nodding that they were okay.

They finished off the last of the biscuits, and visited with Mr. and Mrs. Mouse a little more before heading off. They brushed crumbs from their chins and waved goodbye to the mice.

"Come back real soon!" The mice called down the tunnel.

As they made their way back through the tunnel, Penny felt happy. For the first time in her life, she felt like she was part of a family – like Mr. and Mrs. Mouse had somehow become grandparents to her. It was a warm, good feeling to belong.

After thinking over Mr. Mouse's explanation of the ancient words, Penny turned to Ethan. "Is that why you like that scroll so much?"

"What?" Ethan asked.

"You know, what Mr. Mouse said – that the words made Him feel protected."

Ethan nodded.

"And you wanted to share the words with me so I could feel brave too."

He nodded again.

She walked in silence for a few steps, then looked back at him. 'Thanks Ethan."

Ethan felt happy too. It had been a good idea to share the words with Penny after all. And how great was it that the mice also loved those same words?

As they approached the tunnel exit, they replaced the torches in their holders. They crawled out of the hole and into the laundry room.

It had been about the best day any of them could have hoped for. They'd made new friends, eaten fresh biscuits, and best of all, Max was not home.

Ethan and Penny smiled as they casually made their way across the laundry room floor. They were right in the middle of the room when they heard it.

Keys rattled in the entrance door, and in walked Abigail and her parents.

Ethan and Penny stopped in their tracks. They looked at each other in shock. The family was back already? But it was too soon – and they were across the house from the safety of Abigail's room. How would they get back there without being spotted now?

Just then, one green eye peeked through the crack of the laundry room door.

Max was back.

More From the Author

Kimberly Dawn Rempel writes from Canada, specializing in blogging, editing, and sharing her faith-based insights. She also edits fiction and non-fiction manuscripts for authors and speakers in Canada and abroad.

She can be found at www.kimberlydawnrempel.com and on Facebook at
www.facebook.com/KimberlyDawnRempel/WriterEditor

Abigail Dawn Rempel has a website too at

www.abbythewriter.weebly.com

How I Wrote a Book with my Eight-Year-Old

If you've read The Purse People Adventures and wonder all those how-did-they-do-it questions, this book is the answer.

How does a mom write with a child anyway? How much does the child do and how much does the adult do? Do you publish? How?

We're pulling back the curtain on our process! Book two reveals our real life process, complete with photos and... *gulp* ...first drafts.

We hope you come away encouraged that such a project is completely attainable for you, your students, or your children. We did it and you can too!

59165453R00040

Made in the USA
Charleston, SC
29 July 2016